Arlene Phillips OBE is a world-renowned director and choreographer creating musicals, videos, films, television programming and spectaculars. Her inventive choreography has been seen in the musicals *Grease*, *We Will Rock You*, *Starlight Express*, *The Sound of Music*, *Flashdance* and *The Wizard of Oz*. Her screen work includes the films *Annie* and *Legend*, and the television shows *DanceX* and *Britannia High*. Arlene's videos have starred everyone from Robbie Williams to Elton John, Whitney Houston to Tina Turner. Her largest ever spectacular was the XVII Commonwealth Games. She is known throughout the UK as a former judge on *Strictly Come Dancing* and now on *So You Think You Can Dance?* Her favourite job, however, has been as mother to her two daughters, Alana and Abi.

First published in 2011
by Faber and Faber Limited
Bloomsbury House
74–77 Great Russell Street
London WC1B 3DA

Designed by Baobab Editorial and Design
Printed in England by Bookmarque, Croydon, UK

A CIP record for this book
is available from the British Library

978–0–571–26076–8

2 4 6 8 10 9 7 5 3 1

Stage Sensation

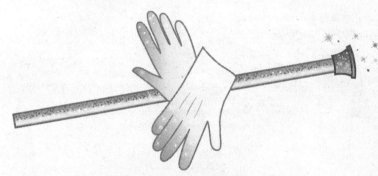

By Arlene Phillips

Illustrated by Pixie Potts

ff

faber and faber

Bracknell
Forest
Council

Miss Trina

Keisha

Matthew

Verity

The Students at Step Out Studio

Alana

Meena

Toby

Chloe

*For Abi, who has always
inspired me*

Chapter 1

'Watch out, Alana!' shouted the teacher.

'Ouch,' yelped Alana, falling over as the netball hit her on the head.

Before she could get up again, Meena grabbed the ball for the opposite team and passed it to the Goal Attack, who scored the winning goal.

The whistle blew. 'Game over!' called the teacher.

As Alana's team filed off the court, she

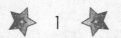

could hear them muttering angrily. 'It's all that Alana's fault,' groaned Thea. 'We would have won if she actually tried to catch the ball instead of staring into space.'

'Leave her alone,' ordered Keisha, the team captain. 'You can't be good at everything. Alana may not be great at netball, but she can dance better than

anyone in the school.'

'Oh, well, that'll come in handy at a netball game,' replied Thea, sarcastically. 'Maybe she could try boogieing round the court – then we're bound to win!'

Alana listened to the conversation miserably, but she didn't say anything. Her head was hurting from where the ball had hit her.

As she was getting changed out of her PE kit, Meena came to sit beside her. 'Never mind,' she said. 'It's only a stupid game.'

Meena's team may have just beaten Alana's at netball, but the two girls were best friends and they certainly weren't going to let something like that come between them.

 3

To Alana's embarrassment, her eyes filled with tears.

'Hey,' called Keisha, coming over. 'What's the matter? You're not crying because of the game, are you? Even I don't think it's *that* important, and netball's my favourite thing!'

'I know it's stupid,' said Alana, her voice shaking a bit. 'But I honestly do try to throw straight and catch the ball and I just can't seem to get the hang of it. And Thea and the others are so mean – it's just making me dread PE lessons.'

'Well, if it's bothering you that much, why don't I help you out with some extra coaching at lunchtimes?' suggested Keisha.

'Would you really?' asked Alana.

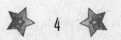

'Sure – why not?' Keisha shrugged. 'It's not like you can't run fast – you're ultra-fit from all the dancing you do. So we just need to work on your hand-eye coordination – that's all.'

'Thanks, Keisha, you're a good friend,' said Alana, wiping her eyes and smiling weakly.

The bell rang for the end of the school day. 'Eek,' squealed Meena. 'We'll have to hurry if we're going to get to Step Out Studio in time. You know what Miss Trina's like if you're late.'

Step Out Studio was the place where Alana, Meena and Keisha went to dance classes. It was Alana's favourite part of the week, by far, because she loved to dance more than anything in the world.

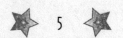

Immediately her face brightened. She quickly flung her sports kits into her locker, grabbed her dance bag and was standing at the door, tapping her feet impatiently before the others had even taken their PE kit off.

Chapter 2

Miss Trina stood at the front of the dance studio, looking as elegant as ever. She wore her cashmere crossover cardigan and her shiny hair was tightly pulled back. She cleared her throat, and immediately all the dance students stopped their warm-up exercises and fell silent.

'Before we start our class today,' said Miss Trina in her clear voice, 'I have an announcement to make.'

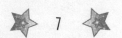

The room suddenly became tense with
expectation and all eyes were on Miss Trina.

'You'll all have heard of the new
hit musical, *Stage Sensation*, that's been
touring the country,' she continued.

There were murmurs of recognition
round the room.

'I've already been to the West End to
see it!' called Verity, smugly.

'Well,' went on Miss Trina, ignoring
the interruption, 'it's going to be coming

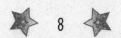

to our town and they need a children's chorus. And this will be made up of students from Step Out Studio.'

There was a huge cheer and everyone started talking at once. Alana and Meena grinned at each other. Dancing in a real musical! How cool was that!

'This is the best thing *ever*,' squealed Keisha, coming up to them. 'I *love* musicals.'

'Oh yeah,' replied Alana. 'I'd forgotten – you're always watching *The Sound of Music*, aren't you?'

'At least once a week!' laughed Keisha. 'And I've got this big book of show tunes I play on the piano. I know loads of the lyrics off by heart. I never thought I'd get to perform in a real musical though!'

Miss Trina let the students talk for a

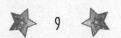

few minutes, then she clapped her hands for silence again.

'I'm going to send out a permission letter to all your parents, which they'll need to sign,' she continued. 'And we'll have to rehearse very hard. I will teach you the moves for the first couple of weeks, then the show's choreographer will be taking over. So we'll start right now, today. Everyone form a straight line and I am going to teach you a step-kick combination. We'll begin by

rehearsing the grand finale, because that's going to be the most difficult piece of choreography.'

Everyone stood in a long line, and Miss Trina put on the soundtrack from *Stage Sensation*. 'Now,' she said, 'follow me: step touch, step kick, right hand to hip and cross feet followed by sharp turn! I want absolute precision. It has to look to the audience as though you are dancing as one, with clean, sharp, precise

moves. Your steps need to be in time, and your kicks all at exactly the same height.'

The students concentrated hard as they danced. They were used to dancing individually or in pairs, and it took a great deal of focus to move at exactly the same time.

Stage Sensation had been in all the papers since it launched in London. Everywhere it went, it played to packed houses night after night. The story was set in the Second World War. It was about a young girl with an incredible voice who travelled round performing to the troops on the battle front. It had just been announced in the papers that there was going to be a new child star of the show – Mirabelle Montague, last year's winner

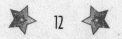

of *Superstar Search*, who'd wowed TV audiences with her amazing singing.

Miss Trina's eyes looked up and down the line of students, and she called out words of praise or criticism as they moved. 'Stay in line, Keisha!' 'Good, Meena!' 'Stretch your supporting knee when you kick, Matthew!' 'Keep your eye on the others, Keisha – this is not a solo – you all need to move as one.'

Miss Trina made them go over the same routine again and again, until, by the end of the lesson, everyone was sweating and exhausted.

As Alana changed back into her jeans after the practice, she could see Keisha on the other side of the row of pegs. She looked upset.

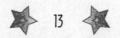

'What's up?' asked Alana quietly. 'I thought you were more excited than any of us about *Stage Sensation*.'

'I am!' whispered Keisha, a catch in her voice. 'That's why I'm upset – I couldn't get anything right in the rehearsal today.'

'But it's only the first rehearsal we've done,' said Alana, reassuringly. 'We've all got loads of time to work on the choreography.'

'Yes,' moaned Keisha, 'but everyone else was so much more together than me. I'm so tall, I just felt like my arms and legs were all over the place.'

'I'm sure you'll get better once we've had a few more rehearsals,' said Alana.

But Keisha didn't look convinced.

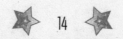

Chapter 3

Two weeks later and Alana was at Step Out Studio to work on *Stage Sensation*. Everyone was tense with anticipation: this was the day the choreographer would take over the rehearsals. And, even more excitingly, Mirabelle Montague, the star of the show and last year's winner of *Superstar Search*, was arriving as well.

The students didn't have to wait long for Mirabelle. Just as they were starting

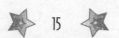

some leg stretches, the double doors of the studio were opened by a mousy-looking woman with a worried expression, and in marched a girl whose face was very familiar from Saturday-night TV. Mirabelle Montague was wearing a pink leather jacket, a white vest top and white trousers. She had huge hoop earrings, white high heels, and a lot of mascara and pink lipstick. She looked much more than twelve years old.

Mirabelle paused in the doorway for effect, a smile hovering round

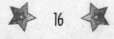

16

her lips as the room fell silent. Then she flounced over to the nearest chair, flung herself into it with a sigh, and announced, 'I need a Coke.'

'Yes, of course, Mirabelle dear,' said the mousy woman, and scuttled out of the room again.

The students were so transfixed with this little drama, they hadn't noticed that someone else had also entered. Miss Trina clapped her hands for silence and Alana turned round. There, next to her, was the smallest woman Alana had ever seen. She had a tiny waist, delicate hands with long fingers, high cheekbones and cropped hair dyed bright red.

'This,' said Miss Trina, 'is Miss Natasha Volkov, the choreographer of *Stage*

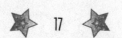

17

Sensation.' Miss Volkov nodded slightly, but did not smile.

'She looks like she might blow over if she went too near an electric fan,' whispered Keisha to Alana.

'And this,' said Miss Trina, beckoning Mirabelle over with a smile, 'is Mirabelle Montague who will be the star of *Stage Sensation.* Please make her feel welcome.'

'Hi everyone!' said Mirabelle. 'Don't be nervous about meeting me. I'm just like all of you, really.'

Meena and Alana glanced at each other, trying not to laugh. Was she being serious?

'Now, everyone into positions please for the dance in Act One!' called Miss Volkov.

Immediately the students ran to their

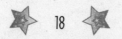

places, all except for Verity who didn't seem to have heard. She was staring at Mirabelle, grinning like mad and trying, but failing, to catch her eye.

Verity was the richest and prettiest girl at Step Out Studio – but she was the nastiest, too. She was jealous of Alana because she was such a great dancer. It looked as though she was very impressed with Mirabelle, though.

A fierce voice rang out across the studio, making everyone jump. 'You there by the window,' shouted Miss Volkov. 'Are you planning to join this rehearsal or not?'

Verity went bright red and ran sheepishly into position.

It didn't take long for the students to

realise that Miss Volkov was someone to
be respected, even though she was so tiny.
Again and again her voice carried across
the room, criticising one student after
another. And it was poor Keisha who
came in for the worst of the comments.

'No, no – raise your arms higher!' cried
Miss Volkov. 'Every time you kick your
lazy legs you are out of time!'

As Alana danced, she glanced at Keisha
out of the corner of her eye and saw that
her eyes were full of tears. All at once,
Alana felt hot in the face. She was angry
at this Miss Volkov who was upsetting
her friend so much. She tried to smile
encouragingly at Keisha, but Keisha
seemed to be in her own world, a strained
expression on her face as she attempted to

move directly in line with the others. Each time Miss Volkov told her off, her dancing seemed to get worse: now even her arms were wrong.

At the end of the lesson, Keisha ran off and shut herself in the props cupboard. Alana followed her and knocked on the door. All she could hear was a muffled

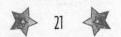

sobbing from inside. She pushed the door open to find Keisha sitting on a pile of feather boas, tears running down her cheeks. Alana squashed in beside her and put an arm around her.

Neither of them said anything for a while. Then Keisha hiccupped something through her tears.

'What was that?' asked Alana.

'I said, Miss Volkov's not going to let me be in the show if I don't get any better.'

Alana squeezed her arm. 'I'm sure she will,' she said, trying to sound confident. But she feared Keisha might be right. Miss Volkov didn't seem like the sort of person to let anyone into her show who wasn't completely up to scratch.

The girls' conversation was interrupted

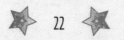

by Verity's voice outside the closed door.

'I think your singing is *amazing*!' she said.

'OK, thanks, whatever,' said Mirabelle's voice.

'No, really!' insisted Verity. 'I watched you through all the audition stages on *Superstar Search* and I knew you were going to win the whole time.'

'Yeah, I knew it too,' replied

Mirabelle, warming up a little bit in the glow of Verity's flattery.

Inside the props cupboard, Keisha gave Alana a wobbly grin. Verity always said *Superstar Search* and shows like it were mindless entertainment – but it turned out she watched it after all.

'Who's that woman you came in with?' continued Verity.

'Oh her? That's Boring Bridget,' replied Mirabelle, dismissively. 'My manager hires her to drive me around and fetch me stuff and things.'

'Wow,' said Verity. 'It must be so cool to have someone to do everything for you.'

The girls' voices faded away as they headed towards the locker rooms. 'I feel sorry for Bridget,' whispered Keisha,

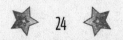

'having to put up with Mirabelle all the time.'

'Me too!' giggled Alana. 'Anyway, let's get changed and get out of here.' They stood up with difficulty in the tiny space, then squeezed out of the cupboard. When they opened the door, Miss Trina was passing right on the other side. She raised her eyebrows when she saw them, but she didn't say anything.

Chapter 4

As the weeks went by, Alana, Keisha and Meena spent almost all their spare time rehearsing for the show, either at Step Out Studio, or by themselves at home. Meanwhile, every lunchtime at school, Keisha took Alana out to work on her netball skills. Gradually Alana was getting better at catching and scoring, and she'd stopped dreading PE lessons.

The same couldn't be said for Keisha

and her rehearsals with Miss Volkov. 'I don't know what to do,' she groaned to Alana. They'd taken a break from netball practice and had flopped down in the school playground, leaning against a wall. 'Miss Trina actually told me after rehearsal yesterday that Miss Volkov won't let me be in the show if I don't improve. It's just not fair. I'm trying soooo hard. I'll feel I've totally let my dad down if I don't get to perform.'

'Oh, I'm sure he'll be OK about it,' replied Alana. 'He'll know you tried your best.'

'Trying my best isn't good enough for him,' sighed Keisha. 'He expects so much of me. He's always asking about what I'm up to, like it all has to be measured.

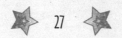

"What marks are you getting at school? How many goals have you scored at netball? When are you going to get an audition for a professional dance part?" It never stops. And if I don't give him the answers he wants, he doesn't say anything. He just looks disappointed, which is worse than getting angry in a way.'

'I can't imagine what that must be

like,' replied Alana, sympathetically. 'My dad's not around at all, and I always think that's rubbish. But maybe it'd be even worse to have a dad who's always pushing you. My mum never expects anything of me except to be at home to look after my sister when she's revising for her exams. She's doing a computing diploma, but she can only study in the evenings because she has to work during the day.'

'Families eh?' sighed Keisha. 'I could do with mine being a bit *less* interested in me, and you want yours to be a bit *more* interested in you.'

Alana nodded. 'Anyway,' she said, 'it's not as if Mirabelle is doing so well in rehearsals either.'

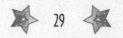

It was true. Although Mirabelle certainly had an amazing singing voice, she was having trouble getting her steps right. She hadn't had the strict dance training of the Step Out Studio students. But what made it worse was that she wouldn't listen to criticism.

'No, Mirabelle,' Miss Volkov would say. 'You must turn your hips like this.'

'I WAS doing that!' Mirabelle would shout, and then she would flounce out of the room. Miss Volkov never said anything – she just watched her go with a steely look in her eye.

Mirabelle is a star, though, thought Alana. She isn't going to be thrown out of the show. But Keisha might be – she actually might. I wish there was

something I could do to help – especially when Keisha's being so great at helping me with netball practice.

Alana sighed. I'll just have to be encouraging and hope that Keisha improves in time for the show.

That evening, as Alana was walking home past Madame Coco's Costume Emporium, the glow from the window seemed to beckon to her. Without really meaning to, she turned and pushed open the door.

Chapter 5

Alana was greeted by the familiar smell –
a mixture of greasepaint and leather and
Madame Coco's perfume. For a moment
she thought the shop was empty – then she
jumped with shock as a rail of costumes
was pushed to one side and Madame
Coco shimmied around it in a burst of
song, her arms held high, her head back.
'*Bright lights on Broadwayyy!*' she warbled.

She didn't notice Alana. Alana cleared

her throat quietly, but Madame Coco was singing too loudly to hear. *'They're coming my wayyy!'* she trilled, spinning round.

'Madame Coco!' called Alana. 'Madame COCO!'

Madame Coco stopped singing abruptly and skidded to a stop. 'Alana, ma chérie!' she exclaimed, not looking at all embarrassed. 'It is so many weeks since I have seen you. I thought you had forgotten me!' She kissed Alana extravagantly on both cheeks.

'Come and sit down, little one. I will make you some lemonade.'

While Madame Coco was fetching Alana's drink, Alana picked up the costumes that had been knocked off the rail during Madame Coco's musical

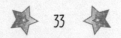

number. Then she sat down in a flowered armchair and gazed around. She never tired of looking at the rows of costumes for every type of dance, the shelves of shoes and sequins, fans and feathers. I wonder, she mused, whether Madame Coco would be able to give me some advice about how to help Keisha with her dancing. She's helped me so many times before.

When Madame Coco returned, she handed Alana some cloudy lemonade in a crystal glass. Then she sat down opposite her.

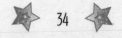

'So, ma petite,' she said. 'You have a worry do you not?'

'I'm sorry, Madame

Coco!' exclaimed Alana. 'You must think
I only come to see you to talk about my
problems. But actually I love just to sit
here and chat with you – and I love your
shop as well.'

'But that is why I am here,' Madame
Coco replied. 'To listen. You can always
tell me what is troubling you.'

'It's my friend Keisha, actually,' sighed
Alana. And she told her all about Keisha's
love of musicals and how much she
wanted to be in *Stage Sensation*, but how
difficult she was finding it to dance in the
chorus line.

Madame Coco listened carefully,
then she closed her eyes and sank into
thought. She stayed like that for so long
that Alana was starting to fear she might

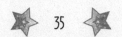

have fallen asleep. But then suddenly she got up and bustled off to the back of the shop. 'I have a costume you must try!' she called as she went. She returned after a moment with a waistcoat and jacket completely covered with gold sequins and an exquisite gold leotard and jewelled tights. They all sparkled so brightly Alana could hardly look at them. She threw them on to Alana's lap. 'Go and put these on,' she ordered.

Obediently, Alana disappeared into the mirrored changing room. She had no idea why Madame Coco wanted her to try on this costume or what it had to do with Keisha's problems. She trusted her, though, and she knew better than to argue.

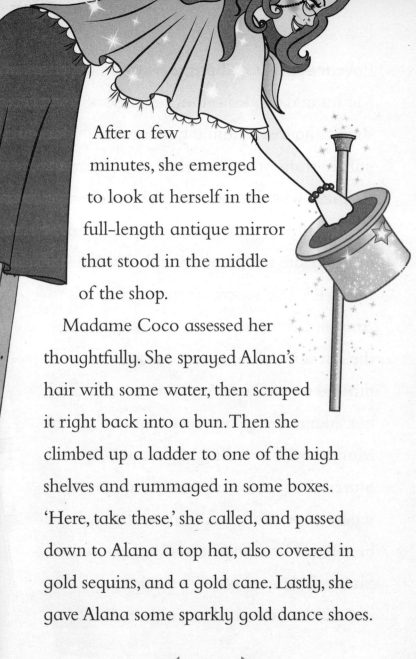

After a few
minutes, she emerged
to look at herself in the
full-length antique mirror
that stood in the middle
of the shop.

Madame Coco assessed her
thoughtfully. She sprayed Alana's
hair with some water, then scraped
it right back into a bun. Then she
climbed up a ladder to one of the high
shelves and rummaged in some boxes.
'Here, take these,' she called, and passed
down to Alana a top hat, also covered in
gold sequins, and a gold cane. Lastly, she
gave Alana some sparkly gold dance shoes.

When Alana had put everything on, Madame Coco looked at her approvingly. 'Now,' she said, 'show me one of the dances from *Stage Sensation*.'

Alana found a space in the middle of the shop floor and, imagining the music in her head, she started the Rockette-style kick line routine from the finale. Almost as soon as she'd started to dance, she felt a whirling sensation and the ground seemed to disappear from under her. Alana closed her eyes. She could hear Madame Coco calling, as though from a great distance, 'Remember, ma petite, when your good deed is done, the call of home will beckon. You will return home! You will return home!'

Still she kept dancing, although it felt

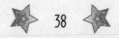

as though there was nothing beneath her feet. Madame Coco's voice faded away and was replaced by some music that sounded familiar, although she couldn't quite place it. She could feel the wooden floor beneath her feet again but she could sense that she was no longer in Madame Coco's shop.

When she opened her eyes, she found herself in a room that she immediately recognised as a theatre dressing room. There were the usual rows of mirrors surrounded by light bulbs. Alana could see herself reflected in them over and over, her gold sequins sparkling. Clothes rails like the ones in Madame Coco's shop held costumes of every description. A long dressing table ran around the

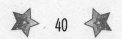

40

wall, cluttered with make-up, face wipes, bottles of lotion and personal belongings – handbags, good-luck cards and mascots.

Looking up, Alana drew in her breath. On a row of hooks at the back of the room were about twenty sets of gold waistcoats and jackets, all exactly like hers. On a shelf above them, gold top hats and canes were piled high.

As Alana stared at them, wondering what it all meant, she heard a muffled sob from behind her. She swung round to see that on a chair in a corner, half hidden by some costumes, there was a girl of about her own age. She was making a peculiar, hoarse hiccuppy sort of noise. Alana eventually worked out she was crying.

Chapter 6

'What's the matter?' asked Alana, drawing the costumes to one side and letting some light into the dark corner. The girl jumped up, startled, and looked at her, blinking a little. Her eyes were rimmed with red as though she'd been crying for a long time.

'*Everything's* the matter,' she croaked,

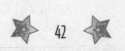

melodramatically. 'I've got laryngitis!' She looked at Alana as though expecting her to say something in reply.

'Er, you've got laryn-what?' asked Alana.

'Gitis!' replied the girl, impatiently. 'I've lost my voice! It means I can't perform tonight! And my understudy is stuck in San Francisco – there's a thick fog so her plane can't take off. She definitely won't get back before tomorrow. And it's impossible to find another child performer at the last minute. The choreographer is *furious* with me, even though it's not my fault.'

'That's so unfair,' said

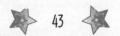

Alana, sympathetically. 'But what show is it?'

'It's *Bright Lights on Broadway* of course!' replied the girl, hoarsely.

'Oh, that's so cool!' exclaimed Alana. 'I saw that a couple of years ago. It was the proper West End production and it came on tour to my town.'

The girl looked at Alana as if she were a bit crazy. '*Bright Lights on Broadway* is a brand-new show,' she said. 'It's the premiere tonight.'

'Oh,' stammered Alana. 'Oh . . . yeah . . . sorry, I must have been remembering something else.'

She thought fast. Where was she? And when? The girl spoke with an American accent so she must be in the USA – and if

this was the premiere of the show then she must be in New York on Broadway itself – the home of musical theatre.

I must have gone back in time, she thought, if this is the show's first night. So what year is it? She didn't want to ask that question in case the girl thought she was crazy. Then her eyes lit up as she spied a newspaper lying on the table

nearby. She wandered over to it, casually, and glanced at the date. 7 June 1986. Alana tried not to panic. It felt really weird to be here when she wouldn't even be born for over ten more years!

'What's the matter?' asked the girl, curiously. 'You look as though you've seen a ghost.'

'Nothing! I'm fine!' Alana replied, trying to sound breezy.

'Anyway,' the girl continued, her eyes narrowing a little. 'Who are you?' She looked Alana up and down, taking in her gold waistcoat and top hat. 'Why are you dressed up in one of our costumes? You don't belong here. Hey! Did you just walk in off the street and barge into our dressing room?'

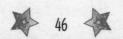

'No, no,' stuttered Alana, desperately trying to work out how to explain herself. 'Erm, you see I've got this friend Keisha at my dance school,' she began, playing for time.

'Dance school?' interrupted the girl. 'You go to dance school?'

'Erm . . . yes,' stammered Alana.

'Have you ever done any musical theatre work?'

'Well, I'm rehearsing for a show at the moment, actually,' Alana replied. 'But I've never performed in a musical before, and I've never sung, except in the shower.'

'It doesn't matter,' said the girl, excitedly. She'd obviously forgotten all about Alana being an impostor. 'What's your name, anyway?' she asked.

 47

'Alana,' said Alana.

'I'm Courtney,' the girl replied. 'Come with me. We're going to see Fabio, the choreographer.' And taking the bemused Alana by the elbow, she dragged her out the door, along a corridor, through the theatre wings and right out on to the stage, where a group of dancers were in mid-rehearsal. Alana stopped short, feeling incredibly self-conscious. Fabio was a tall, very good-looking young man with piercing blue

eyes and an annoyed expression. He glanced up at them and raised his hand to stop the dancers. 'What is it, Courtney?' he demanded impatiently. 'Who's this? What's she doing in my theatre?'

Hearing how cross he sounded, Alana felt even more nervous. What have you got me into now, Madame Coco? she thought to herself.

'This is Alana,' croaked Courtney. 'I think she may be able to understudy me tonight.'

Fabio strode across the stage and up to Alana, staring at her with his intense eyes. 'Who are you?' he demanded. 'What makes you think you can take part in my show?'

'I d–d–don't,' Alana started to stammer,

49

but then Courtney interrupted.

'She goes to dance school. She looks my age. She has a costume that fits. Surely it's worth a try?'

'For this part, you must be able to sing as well as dance,' said Fabio to Alana. 'Do you sing?'

'No, not really,' Alana replied.

Fabio turned back to Courtney. 'So, this is verrrry helpful,' he said sarcastically. 'First you go and lose your voice on the day of the premiere. Then you bring me a girl, a complete stranger, who does not sing.'

'She does dance, though,' Courtney replied.

'Let me see you dance,' Fabio ordered. 'Cue the music!'

Only then did Alana notice that an

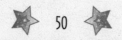

entire band was there, in the orchestra
pit. They struck up the chords of the
final scene of *Bright Lights on Broadway*.
Hesitantly, Alana began to dance. To her
amazement, she found her feet knew the
steps to the routine, even though she'd
never done it before. She was so swept
up in the music that she forgot to worry

about Fabio viewing her closely, not
to mention the entire chorus who were
sitting on the edge of the stage, watching
the whole scene with enormous interest.

'Hmmm, not bad,' said Fabio,
grudgingly, as the music drew to a close.
'Now let's hear your voice.'

Nervously, Alana sang a few bars of
one of the songs. She knew the whole
soundtrack off by heart, but her singing
wasn't that great.

Fabio held up his hand to stop her. 'We
have work to do if we are to get you up
to scratch by tonight,' he declared.

'So's she's got the part?' asked Courtney,
excitedly.

'Yes, for one night, till your real
understudy can get here,' Fabio replied.

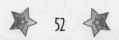

'We have six hours until the curtain goes up. I want two hours of intensive voice coaching for her, then I will take her for a one-to-one rehearsal.'

He turned round to face the other dancers. 'Then I want everyone back here at four p.m. for another dress rehearsal. Cast dismissed!'

Chapter 7

Before Alana knew it, she was being ushered off by a blonde woman to a room behind the stage containing a piano. 'I am Giselle, the voice coach,' explained the woman.

Giselle looked Alana up and down, frowning at the waistcoat and sparkly tights. She was still clutching the top hat and cane. 'You do not need to be in costume you know,' she said. 'Run back

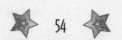

to the dressing room and change into
your normal clothes, then come straight
back here.'

Alana dashed off to the dressing
room, panicking. She didn't have any
normal clothes! They were on the floor
of Madame Coco's dressing room, 3,000
miles away and over twenty years in the
future! She couldn't quite believe this was
happening. No one had even asked her if
she *wanted* to take part in the show.

Courtney was in the dressing room,
chatting with one of the other girls.

'What's the matter?' she asked Alana as
she came flying in.

'Giselle says I have to change out
of my costume, but I don't have any
normal . . . er . . . I can't find my normal

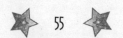

clothes,' Alana explained.

'Oh, that's OK,' Courtney replied. 'It's easy to lose things in this tip of a dressing room! You can borrow these jeans and a T-shirt – they're spares. I've got some trainers you can wear, too. You look about my size.'

Impulsively, Alana hugged Courtney. 'You're a star!' she said.

'I wish,' croaked Courtney, gloomily. 'It's you who are going to be the star tonight!'

When Alana arrived back at the practice room, Giselle was sitting ready at the piano.

'Now, sing a G major scale,' she commanded. She played a single note, then looked at Alana expectantly.

Alana stared back. 'Erm, what is it you wanted me to do again?' she asked Giselle.

'A G major scale,' repeated Giselle patiently. 'Like this.' And she played it on the piano.

Alana did the best she could to copy what she'd heard.

'Hmmmm. We're going to have to

work hard,' said Giselle.

There followed two hours of some of the most intense work Alana had ever done. She learned breathing exercises. She sang scale after scale. She practised voice projection and breathing from her diaphragm, as well as working on the lyrics so she understood the meaning of every word she had to sing. They sang until Alana felt she was about to lose her voice, just like Courtney! Luckily, it was one of Alana's favourite musicals, so she already knew a lot of the lyrics off by heart.

I bet I don't know them as well as Keisha does, she thought.

As soon as Alana's voice coaching was over, she was taken back to the stage where Fabio was waiting for her. He

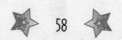

made Alana dance every routine she was involved in, singing at the same time. He sat in the auditorium, staring at her, his piercing eyes unsmiling, only speaking when he had a criticism to make. Alana found him absolutely terrifying, although curiously charming at the same time.

By the time the full dress rehearsal was due to start, Alana was starting to feel on top of things. Courtney came to stand in the wings to watch. She gave Alana an encouraging thumbs-up as she took her position with the rest of the chorus.

As Alana sang and danced, it felt as if she was moving as one body with the others. Her heart leapt and she began to enjoy herself and to relax into the part.

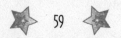

At last Fabio called a halt to the rehearsal. 'One hour for dinner, everybody!' he declared. 'Then back to the theatre please.'

Courtney smiled at Alana as she trooped off the stage with the others. 'My mom's taking me for a burger before the show,' she croaked. 'Wanna come?'

'Oh, er, I don't have any money,' Alana replied, embarrassed.

'Don't worry – it's on me. You've completely saved my life with Fabio today.'

Courtney's mother was waiting for her at the stage door. As soon as Courtney explained who Alana was, she greeted her with delight. 'You come along with us,' she said. 'You're gonna need some good feeding up before the show.'

They walked down the road from the theatre, then turned the corner. All at once, Alana was overwhelmed by the glittering lights of Times Square, New York. Her guess had been right – she was on Broadway. She began to feel terrified all over again, but excited, too.

'I'm about to perform in the premiere of one of the best-loved musicals there's ever been, on Broadway, the world capital of musical theatre,' she muttered to herself. 'Broadway! This is just a dream come true. My mum would surely be proud if she could see me now.'

'What was that?' Courtney's mother asked kindly.

'Oh, er, nothing.' Alana blushed.

The three of them went into the nearest burger restaurant, and both girls chose a Triple Cheesy Wham Burger with large fries and a strawberry milkshake. Alana was absolutely starving after her afternoon's work, and Courtney's laryngitis didn't seem to have affected her appetite either – or her conversation for

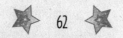

that matter. She was incredibly talkative. Luckily she had so much to say that it didn't occur to either her or her mum to ask Alana who she was, or where she'd come from.

In her croaky voice, Courtney told Alana that she was twelve – a year older than me, Alana thought – and went to middle school. She loved roller-blading and trampolining, but since she'd got the part in this show she hadn't had time to do either of them – and she'd barely been able to see her friends, either. She thought it was worth it though. A girl in her class had gone for the same part and hadn't got it, so now she kept saying mean things about Courtney to her friends. But Courtney didn't care because she knew

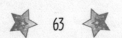

the other girl was only jealous.

Alana smiled and nodded and chewed. I'm not convinced she's got laryngitis, she thought to herself. I think she's just talked her voice into oblivion!

The girls barely had time to finish off their meal with some jam doughnuts before it was time to head back to the theatre.

As they walked through the crowds of shoppers and traffic fumes towards the theatre, Alana began to feel terrified all over again.

The girls parted at the stage door. Courtney gave Alana a good-luck hug. 'Thank you soooo much for doing this for me,' she said. 'I'll be watching from the wings!' Alana gave her a nervous smile.

The next hour seemed to pass in a daze. Alana joined the other chorus girls in the dressing room. She put her gold outfit back on and one of the older girls showed her how to do her make-up. Then they all trooped on to the stage for some warm-up exercises. One of them peeped around the curtain. 'The seats are starting to fill up,' she reported. Alana's heart seemed to do a somersault. She almost wished the show was starting right now, so she could get it over with.

The time came soon enough. Alana waited in the wings as the orchestra began the overture. Then, smiling and looking at the audience as she'd been taught, she danced on to the stage in perfect time with the rest of the chorus, singing the opening

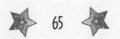

number and trying hard to remember
all the breathing and voice-projecting
techniques she'd been taught.

By the interval, Alana had started to
relax and enjoy herself. 'You're doing really
well,' said Courtney as Alana downed a
whole bottle of water in one go.

By the final curtain call, she had
pretty much decided on a career in

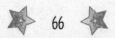

musical theatre! The audience gave
everyone a standing ovation, whooping
and cheering, and demanding curtain
call after curtain call. As Alana bowed
again and again, her heart seemed to be
beating at twice its usual speed. I think
this might be the best night of my life
ever! she thought to herself.

As soon as the curtain fell for the last

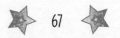

time, Fabio came up and kissed her on either cheek. 'You were a real star tonight, Alana,' he said. It was the first time Alana had seen him smile, and she felt slightly weak at the knees. Fabio handed her a brown envelope, and before she had time to thank him or ask what it was, she heard some familiar words, as though from a great distance:

'Remember, ma petite, when your good deed is done, the call of home will beckon. You will return home! You will return home!'

The boards of the stage disappeared, and with them the buzz of the audience filing out of the auditorium. Alana closed her eyes, and Madame Coco's words became louder and closer, until

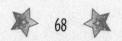

she could hear them right next to her.
Opening her eyes, she found herself back
in Madame Coco's shop. She glanced at
the grandfather clock just to check. Yes,
as usual no time had passed here since
her adventure had started. No one would
have missed her.

'That was the most fantastic night of
my life, Madame Coco,' she said. 'Thank
you!' And she went into the fitting room
to change back into her own clothes.

'Come and see me again soon, ma
chérie,' said Madame Coco as Alana
handed her back the costume. Alana gave
her a hug, then she left the shop and ran
down the road to her house, still glowing
with the excitement of the show.

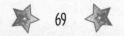

Chapter 8

The next morning, Alana walked to school in a bit of a daze. She could still hardly believe the adventure she'd just had.

The trouble is, she thought, I don't see how it can help Keisha. I shouldn't expect Madame Coco to be able to solve everyone's problems, though – it's not fair.

When Alana entered her classroom, Keisha came running up to her. 'My mum says do you want to come back to

mine after school?'

'Yeah, I'd love to!' Alana replied. She'd never been round to Keisha's before. 'I'll have to check with my mum, but I know she's around to look after Abi this evening so it should be fine.'

Alana and Keisha caught the bus together after school. They got off in a part of town Alana hadn't been to before. The houses were much bigger than the ones she was used to seeing. The gardens were manicured, the pavements free of litter; even the trees seemed to have shinier leaves.

'Here we are,' said Keisha, turning into a driveway. Alana tried to hide her amazement. The whole of the front of the house was made of glass. You could see

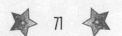

the big kitchen on the ground floor all lit up, with Keisha's mum sitting at the table drinking coffee.

Alana had no idea that Keisha's family was so wealthy. They both went to the same ordinary school, and, unlike Verity, Keisha had never said anything to show that her family were well off.

When Keisha introduced Alana, her mum kissed her on both cheeks.

The girls sat down at the breakfast bar. Keisha's mum gave them each a glass bottle of Coke with a straw in it, popping off the cap with a silver bottle opener.

Up in Keisha's bedroom later, Alana flopped down in a pink beanbag chair.

'Let's put on some music,' said Keisha. She had a Bose iPod dock in her room

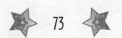

and she switched on the soundtrack to
Bright Lights on Broadway. Alana smiled to
herself – little did Keisha know that she
had just performed in the premiere! As
soon as the first number started, Keisha
began singing along.

'Wow, Keisha,' exclaimed Alana when
the track came to an end. 'Your voice is
brilliant – I had no idea!'

'Oh, it's not really,' replied Keisha,
blushing. 'I've never had any professional
training or anything – I just enjoy
singing. I sing all the time at home – it
drives my sisters nuts.'

'I'd give anything to be able to sing like
that,' Alana replied.

But Keisha was embarrassed by Alana's
enthusiasm and stopped singing. Nothing

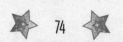

could persuade her to carry on, however much Alana begged her. So the girls spent the rest of the evening gossiping about school until Keisha's mum came in to tell Alana it was time to drive her home.

Chapter 9

There were only two weeks left until the opening night. As soon as Alana came through the door of Step Out Studio for the rehearsal, she knew something was wrong. Miss Volkov was standing talking to Miss Trina, and her face was like thunder. Near them was Bridget, looking scared and wringing her hands in a helpless sort of way. Mirabelle was not with her.

'What's going on?' Alana whispered to Chloe, who was already there.

'It's Mirabelle,' Chloe whispered back. 'Apparently, she's not coming today. I heard Bridget pass on a message to Miss Volkov from her. She says that she isn't going to bother with any more rehearsals before the first night, because she's good enough already.'

Alana was shocked. 'But her dancing isn't even that great!' she murmured. 'Miss Volkov's always correcting her steps and she never seems to listen.'

'It must be hard for Mirabelle,' sighed Chloe. 'After all, the rest of us at Step Out Studio have been dancing together for so long, and she probably feels left out. Maybe she's too nervous to come to rehearsals.'

Alana just smiled. Chloe always saw the best in everyone, which made her very likeable if not always very perceptive.

Before they had time to discuss the matter any more, Miss Volkov clapped her hands to start the rehearsal. Nothing was said about Mirabelle not being there.

Out of the corner of her eye, Alana could see that Keisha still wasn't managing to keep in time with the complex rhythms and the sharp head moves of the other dancers. Miss Volkov didn't make any comments, though – she just glanced at her now and again.

Maybe she's going to let Keisha go ahead and perform after all, Alana thought to herself with relief.

But as soon as the rehearsal finished, Miss Volkov called, 'Keisha, please come into Miss Trina's office!'

Alana's heart sank. She sat in the changing rooms, waiting for Keisha to come out again. Five minutes later she appeared, tears streaming down her cheeks. Alana ran up to her, ignoring the

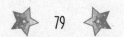 79

curious stares of the other students. She didn't need to ask what had happened – it was obvious that she'd been told she couldn't take part in the show.

'It's not fa-a-a-ir,' sobbed Keisha into Alana's shoulder. 'I wanted to be in this musical more than anything in the wo-o-o-rld.'

By the time Alana had comforted Keisha and persuaded her to change back into her everyday clothes, everyone else had gone home. Just as the two girls were about to leave the changing rooms, they heard Miss Volkov's voice outside the door.

'I cannot work with Mirabelle Montague,' she was saying. 'I have never worked with such a spoiled, unprofessional, and arrogant performer in my life.'

80

Alana and Keisha stared at each other, their eyes wide. Miss Volkov would never be talking like this if she knew there were still students in the building overhearing everything she was saying.

Then came Miss Trina's worried voice. 'I agree with you,' she replied. 'But what can we do? It's only two weeks till the show and there isn't anyone else who could possibly star in it.'

Suddenly, Alana had an brilliant idea. Without even knowing she was going to do it, she burst out of the changing rooms, making Miss Volkov and Miss Trina nearly jump out of their skins. 'I know who can be the new star!' she cried. 'Keisha can!'

'No, she can't!' squeaked Keisha. 'I

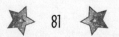

mean, no, I can't!'

Alana turned to Keisha. 'Yes, you can,' she said more calmly. 'Think about it. You're an amazing singer – don't say you aren't, because I've heard you, remember? You know every song in the show off by heart. You can learn the dance routines quickly – you've been watching Mirabelle

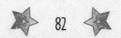

do them for weeks, so that will give you a head start. And you don't have to worry about dancing precisely with the rest of the chorus, because you'll be the soloist!'

She turned to the two teachers. 'Please say you'll give Keisha a chance!' she begged.

Miss Volkov looked doubtful.

'Pleeeease!' Alana repeated.

Miss Volkov sighed. 'Come back here at eight a.m. tomorrow,' she said to Keisha. 'You can audition for me and we will see how you sing.' And she turned round and marched back into the office. Miss Trina smiled at the girls, then followed her.

'You're crazy!' hissed Keisha, as soon as they were alone. 'I can't possibly do this! I've never had a singing lesson in my life!'

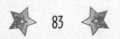

'But I have,' Alana replied, thinking of the voice training she'd had in New York. 'And there are lots of techniques I can teach you. We're going to have to work all evening though.'

Alana persuaded Keisha to phone her parents to get permission to go back to Alana's place. Then they headed off on foot. As they passed Madame Coco's Costume Emporium, Alana smiled to herself. Thanks, Madame Coco! she thought. If I can use what I learned on Broadway to train Keisha well enough to get the part, then my adventure will have helped her after all.

Chapter 10

When Alana opened the front door, she found her mother waiting for her, looking stressed.

'There you are at last!' she said, crossly. 'You were meant to be home ages ago to look after Abi, so I could study.'

Alana sighed. She'd completely forgotten she was supposed to be babysitting Abi that evening. Now she would have her little sister there while

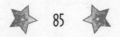

she was trying to coach Keisha.

Abi followed Alana and Keisha into Alana's bedroom. 'You're going to have to be *completely* quiet!' Alana said to her little sister sternly. Then her face softened as she had an idea. 'If you're really *really* good, I'll show you around backstage after the first night of the show.'

'I will be, I promise I promise!' squeaked Abi.

'Right,' said Alana, turning to Keisha. 'We only need to work on one song for your audition.' They decided on a track called 'Singing for Victory'. Alana made Keisha sing it over and over again, practising all the techniques Alana had learned.

'*I'll sing to each father, each brother, each son.*

I'll sing and I'll sing till the battle is won!'
went Keisha.

Alana put up a hand to stop her. 'Now,
let's hear that again,' she said, 'but this
time make sure to breathe from your
diaphragm.'

Abi sat on the bed, watching but not
saying a word.

'How did you even learn about voice coaching?' asked Keisha as the girls stopped for a break and a drink of orange juice.

'Oh, I've had the odd lesson and I picked up some tips from watching *Superstar Search*,' Alana replied vaguely. 'Anyway, we'd better carry on practising,' she added briskly, keen to change the subject.

Keisha and Alana practised all evening, stopping only so Alana could make the three of them a quick sandwich. At last Keisha's dad called to say that it was late and he was coming to fetch her.

'I'll be at Step Out Studio tomorrow morning to cheer you on!' said Alana as she waved goodbye.

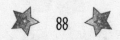 88

'You're a real friend, Alana,' Keisha replied. 'Thank you soooo much for everything, even if I don't get this part!'

Keisha need not have worried. When she sang for Miss Volkov the next morning, the choreographer looked quietly impressed. 'We are going to have to work hard,' she said as Keisha finished the song. 'I will have to give you private coaching each day to learn the solo routines, and I'm going to send you to a professional voice coach to improve your technique.'

'You mean I've got the part?' asked Keisha.

Miss Volkov smiled, and her stern face took on a sudden warmth. 'Yes, you have. I will phone Mirabelle's agent now and

inform her that Mirabelle's services are no longer required.'

But Keisha didn't wait to hear what she was saying. She rushed out of the room to where Alana was waiting in the changing rooms. 'I got it! I got it! I really got it!' she shouted, spinning Alana round and round. 'My dad is going to be sooo proud!'

'Never mind your dad – *you* should be proud of yourself!' grinned Alana.

Laughing and talking non-stop, the two girls headed off to school.

Chapter 11

Alana felt on a high the whole day. She was so thrilled for Keisha. Then things got even better when, during the netball lesson, she managed to score three goals in a row. The teacher came up to her after the lesson, smiling.

'I don't know what's come over you, Alana,' she said, 'but in less than a term you've turned from one of the worst netball players in the class to one of the best.'

Alana looked embarrassed. 'It's down to Keisha,' she explained. 'She's been coaching me in the school playground.'

'Well, whoever it's down to, you've done very well. In fact, I want to ask you to try out for the team.'

Alana's heart leapt. It would be so much fun to play in a school team, going to matches at the weekends, and having extra practices after school, and . . .

Then her face fell. There was no way that she could manage it. She had to spend so much time looking after Abi that it was all she could do to persuade her mum to let her go to Step Out Studio – never mind play extra netball as well.

'I'm sorry, Miss,' she sighed, looking gloomy. 'I'd love to, but things are difficult

at home, you know . . .'

The teacher did know something of Alana's home situation, so she didn't argue. 'It's a shame, though,' she said. 'I think you have great potential.'

Alana sighed as she walked away. Then she pulled herself together. I've got my dancing after all, she thought, and that's the thing that *really* matters to me.

After school there was another show rehearsal. They were almost every evening, now that the opening night was so close.

The first thing that Miss Trina did was to announce that Keisha was taking Mirabelle's part. Verity looked white with fury.

'I can't believe anyone thinks that *you* could be good enough to play a starring

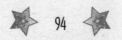

role!' she hissed to Keisha in the changing room afterwards, and she stormed out. Keisha looked upset.

'Don't listen to her,' said Alana. 'You were great tonight. And if Miss Volkov thinks you can do it, that's all you need to know.'

'Verity's only annoyed because she wanted to be friends with Mirabelle, because she's famous,' added Meena. 'And now she won't get the chance.'

Keisha gave a wobbly smile. 'Thanks, girls,' she said. 'It

makes a real difference to know you're supporting me.'

That evening, Alana went up to her room to get ready for bed, singing snatches of *Bright Lights on Broadway* to herself. She felt exhausted by the hectic day, but contented, too. Her friend Keisha was going to star in a musical and she had helped her achieve that. And she had her own amazing New York adventure to remember as well. She thought of Courtney, and the other girls, and Fabio with his intense blue eyes and the smile he'd given her at the end of the show.

As she was getting into her pyjamas, Alana spotted something sticking out from under her bed. Crouching down, she drew out a brown envelope. Of course! she

thought. It's the envelope Fabio gave me after the curtain call!

When Alana had arrived home from Madame Coco's, she'd shoved the envelope under the bed to make sure her mum and sister didn't see it – then she'd forgotten all about it. She pulled it out and brushed off a layer of dust, then she drew out of it a glossy booklet. It was a Playbill for the premiere of *Bright Lights on Broadway*. Inside it was a slip of paper, typed with the following message:

> TONIGHT, for one night only,
> the part of Chorus Girl
> Number 12 will be played
> by eleven-year-old
> ALANA MILNE

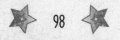

And scrawled across the back, in black felt-tip, was a message just for her.

Alana read it, then blushed, then read it again. She hugged the programme for a minute, then she drew out the purple

Swan Lake

and gold album that Madame Coco had given her to stick in the souvenirs of her adventures. She slipped the programme into one of the cardboard pockets. Then finding a silver pen, she inked music notes all over the outside of the pocket.

When she'd finished, she drew the programme out, to read the message once again:

To Alana, Dancing Star - you saved the show. Thank you! Love Fabio xxx.

Enter Arlene's World of Dance . . .

Become a Broadway star!

Imagine you're dancing on Broadway, just like Alana. These spectacular moves will help you perfect a sensational stage show!

High kick

Take a small step forward and kick high with your other leg. Keep front leg and back straight.

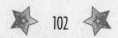

Jazz pirouette

Step forward on your left leg, bring right knee up and turn to your left. Arms join in front to help you round.

Attitude leap

Take a few steps to run up, then leap with front leg straight, back leg bent in 'attitude'. Arms out straight!

Sensational Stage Facts!

Musical theatre dancing is highly energetic and even acrobatic. It is characterised by its use of high kicks, turns and leaps. The chorus plays an important role in creating drama on the stage. They are required to perform precise, intricate movements at the same time. It is a very demanding form of dance.

Theatre dancing has roots in music hall, vaudeville and cabaret,

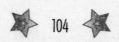

as well as opera. Musicals continued
to develop using contemporary
music and dance styles, such as the
swing dancing and rock'n'roll
in *Grease* and Disco Hustles in
Saturday Night Fever.

Famous stage choreographers
include Jerome Robbins who created
the ballet-inspired *West Side Story*.
Bob Fosse's angular style of
jazz dancing was hugely influential.
He used lots of isolation movements
and often used props such as
canes, hats and chairs, seen
spectacularly in *Cabaret*.

Out now!
Collect all six
Alana Dancing Star
adventures . . .